# Tim McGraw's

# LOVE
## Your Heart

To

From

Date

Published in Nashville, Tennessee, by Tommy Nelson. Tommy Nelson is a trademark of Thomas Nelson, Inc.

Cover and interior design by Koechel Peterson & Associates, Minneapolis, MN.

ISBN: 978-1-4003-1473-7

Printed at RR Donnelley Reynosa,
Tamaulipas, Mexico
January 2010

# Tim McGraw's
# LOVE
## Your Heart

## Tim McGraw
## & Tom Douglas
### Illustrated by Abigail Marble

Tommy
NELSON

A Division of Thomas Nelson Publishers

NASHVILLE  DALLAS  MEXICO CITY  RIO DE JANEIRO

Dedicated to all the families and members of the
United States Armed Forces. Thank you for
courageously serving and protecting our country.
Tim McGraw

For Katie, Katherine, Claire, and Tommy—
may you know "the breadth and length
and height and depth" of true love.
Tom Douglas

Tim and I are so blessed with our three daughters . . . Gracie, Maggie, and Audrey. Our girls all have unique and individual talents:

Gracie—"I love to come up with new recipes and cook for my family."

Maggie—"I love cross-country running and making jewelry with my sisters for my Save Africa project."

Audrey—"I love to sing and hang out with my family."

They are also each kind, caring, and loving. As parents it is gratifying to see this. We all strive to nurture our children's spirits. I love this book because it focuses not only on what children can do, but also who they are on the inside. The girls and I hope that you enjoy this book as much as we have.

**Faith Hill and Gracie, Maggie, and Audrey McGraw**

"Hi, Daddy."

Katie twirled into the kitchen.

"Yum! Chocolate-chip pancakes with whipped cream and blueberry syrup!" she cheered. "It's the perfect breakfast for a decision-making day."

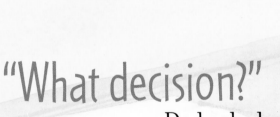

"What decision?"

Dad asked.

"The School Talent Show is next week, and I don't know what to do."

"Don't worry. I'll help you
    find a spectacular talent,"
Dad offered.

"But, Daddy, I have too many talents!
I could do cartwheels, or hula hoop,
    or whistle, or stand on my head.
Which should I choose?"

"Wait! I have a great idea,"
Katie said excitedly.

"I'll teach Palio to juggle.

Okay, Palio, pay attention. Put this egg

in your right paw . . . and toss it to your left.

Uh-oh!"

SPLAT!

Dad laughed.

"Katie, I love your juggling act.

But I think Palio wishes

you would find a

**different talent!**"

"I know!" Katie proclaimed.
"I will do a perfect cartwheel for my talent."

Outside, Katie got a running start, then threw her legs into the air
in a perfect cartwheel V . . .

"Watch out for the PUDDLE!" Dad yelled.
But it was too late.

A very muddy Katie looked up and grinned.

"I love your cartwheels, but go get cleaned up
and try to think of something for the talent show
that isn't so messy," Dad teased.

"How about music?" Katie suggested. "I could sing."

"Great idea," Dad agreed.

"I'll sing the song I wrote for Palio," Katie said.

*"Palio is brown and white.*
*I love him with all my might.*
*Upstairs, downstairs; outside, in,*
*Palio's my bestest friend."*

"Oh, I love your singing more than Palio's howling!" Dad said.

"Daddy, I've tried things all day.
Maybe I don't have as many talents as I thought."
Katie frowned.

"It's okay, God gave you lots of talents, Katie.
Let's ask Him to help you find just
the right one for the Talent Show.

"Whatever you choose, remember,
Mom and I are your biggest fans.

I love you, my little girl."

"Love you more, Daddy.
Come on, Palio. Let's practice our juggling...."

"Palio? Palio?
Now, where did he go?"

On the night of the Talent Show,
Katie and Palio were waiting backstage
when Katie saw Sophie crying.

"What's wrong, Sophie? Are you afraid?"

"No. I'm just sad. I've practiced all year
to beat the school jump-rope record.
This morning I fell and hurt my hand,
and I can't hold the rope.
So, I have to drop out!"
Sophie said.

Katie hugged her friend. Suddenly she knew what
she should do for the Talent Show.

"Don't worry, Sophie. I have an idea!
I'll be right back."

Katie peeked out from the curtain and motioned for Dad.

"Daddy, I need to tell you something,"
Katie whispered.

"Ladies and Gentlemen,
we have a slight change in our program,"
said Principal Mulgrew.

"Katie and her
amazing dog, Palio,
will not be performing
their juggling act.
**Instead,** they will be
joining Sophie Madison."

"196...197...198...199...200!
Hooray for Sophie!"
squealed Katie.

"I believe we have a Talent Show winner!"
announced Principal Mulgrew.

"Sophie Madison, come get your crown!"

Everyone cheered!

After the show, Katie asked softly,
"Daddy are you disappointed,
that I didn't do anything in the Talent Show?"

"Oh, my little girl, you *did* do something!
Showing kindness *is* the best talent of all.
I love your heart, Katie."

"Come on, Palio, let's treat Katie and Sophie to pizza," Dad said.

"Yippee!" shouted Sophie.

"Can I wear my crown?"

"Yes! It looks perfect on you!" Katie smiled.

After pizza, they took Sophie home.

"Thank you for the treat," she said. "And Katie...
I wouldn't have won today if it weren't for you and Palio.
Would you do one more thing for me?"

"Sure. What is it?" asked Katie.

"Would you keep the crown?
It's my gift to you."

"Oh, Sophie. Thank you," said Katie.

"Katie girl, you are beautiful from the outside in",

Dad said.

"I love your juggling.

I love your cartwheels.

I love the funny things you do.

But most of all, I love your heart."

"We hope this book inspires Dads and Daughters to spend time together just being Dads and Daughters. Please feel free to write your own story or special 'love you more' moment in the space below."

Tim and Tom